The Ant with Red Pants

J. A. Osowski

with illustrations by
Michael and Alicia Smith

BALTIC
BOOKS

"Building Self Esteem in Children"

Baltic Books
P. O. Box 706
Baltic CT 06330

ISBN 13: 978-1-5997197-4-0

Printed in the United States of America

To my granddaughters,
Kristy and Amanda.

Also a special thanks for
my wife Ann Marie and
for her motivation and love
to accomplish this dream.

An honorable thanks to the
Veterans Administration Vocational Rehab Dept.
To Sue Fitzgibbons and Don Dobruck for their
assistance to acquire the funds
and for their courteous help.

Also thanks to Dennis Twiss of the
Connecticut Small Business Administration
and for his expertise in the business field.

There once was an ant hill, deep in the forest,
And inside it lived hundreds of ants.

There were workers and soldiers, and one ruling Queen,
But only one single ant that wore pants.

The ant's name was Andrew and he hated his legs,
He knew they were thin and not strong.
But you can be strong without great big muscles,
So Andrew was entirely wrong.

Now ants can lift ten times their own weight
With legs that are short, thin or tall.
Andrew's legs were just like any other ant,
So his legs didn't matter at all.

But poor little Andrew believed he was weak,
Not like his sisters and brothers.
"They're so lucky to be strong," Andrew had thought,
"I wish I could be like the others."

"I can't possibly lift too much with these legs,
They're too skinny," he thought every day.
So he would only carry a small piece of food,
And he would hide when it came time to play.

One day as he gathered the food on the ground,
Apart from the rest of the ants.
He got an idea, to cover his legs,
With a small pair of four legged pants.

He made them from a spider's spun web,
And dyed them with red berry juice.
He held them on with an old rubber band
Because they fit baggy and loose.

The other ants giggled at Andrew's red pants
That he wore twenty four hours a day.
He looked very silly, wearing his pants,
Because ants don't wear clothes anyway.

Then one autumn day, the Queen sent for Andrew,
And he knelt in front of her throne.
"I'm concerned about a serious matter,
You have created, all on your own."

"Now all the ants are making fun of your pants,
They are laughing and fooling around.
They bring back less food at the end of the day
And they leave much more food on the ground."

"So Andrew, I command you, as the Royal Queen ant,
Take off those baggy red pants, right away!
Our Colony will not waste any more time,
Because the frost will come any day."

"Oh please, my great Queen," the little ant said,
As he took off his baggy red pants.
I'm embarrassed to be seen with my four skinny legs,
I just can't face those hundreds of ants."

The Queen looked down at the little black ant,
As he kneeled on his four skinny knees.
"We all work together, to store food for the winter,
Not for you to do as you please!"

NURSERY

"For the sake of all your brothers and sisters,
You must get rid of your pants.....right away!
We all must work, to find enough food,
From sun-up to sun-down, each day."

"You can lift as much food as any other ant,
Without those silly red pants that you wear.
So tomorrow go back to work with the others
And carry a worker-ant's share!"

Early the next day, the ants left the anthill,
They moved quickly through the weeds and the grass.
Over and under the sticks and the rocks,
With Andrew following last.

They were silent and quiet as they hurried about,
Searching for food on the ground.
They scurried up trees and in bushes and stumps,
Wherever any food could be found.

Andrew the ant picked up some food,
Keeping up with the rest of the ants.
He would prove to the Queen that he was a hard worker,
Even without his baggy red pants.

He looked like the hundreds of other small ants,
With feelers and legs and a head.
His body was the same color and shape,
But without the small pants that were red.

When that cold day in autumn finally arrived,
To close the anthill's front door.
The ants had some trouble blocking the hole,
The dirt would crumble and fall on the floor.

THRONE ROOM ↑
NURSERY ↑
GREAT HALL →

They stuffed it with leaves and pieces of paper.
They stuffed it with twigs and with moss.
But all of the stuff just wouldn't work,
And tonight was autumn's first frost.

"I have just what you need", said Andrew the ant.
"I'll be back in a short little bit!"
He ran down the long dark, winding dirt tunnel
While the others decided to sit.

TO
LIVING QUARTERS →

After a minute or so they heard a faint sound
As Andrew huffed and puffed as he ran.
Then Andrew appeared in the long dirt made tunnel,
With his baggy red pants in his hand.

THRONE ROOM ↑
NURSERY ↑
GREAT HALL →

He ran up to the hole with his pants in the air
And tried to squeeze them into the spot.

The other ants joined in and they all pushed together
As the tunnel, became gradually dark.

The small fireflies lit up the tunnel,
And the ants cheered for Andrew the ant.
Even the Queen thought he was truly amazing,
For stuffing the hole with his pants.

THRONE ROOM ↑
NURSERY ↑
GREAT HALL →

The entire ant colony gathered in the Great Hall,
To honor the "Ant of the Season."

They all had voted for Andrew the ant,
And all for the very same reason.

He sat at a table as "Guest Ant of Honor"
While hundreds of ants stretched to see.
But all that they saw was an ant like themselves,
And that's all... Andrew wanted to be.

JOSEPH OSOWSKI

Joseph resides in Eastern Connecticut with his wife Ann Marie. Joseph and Ann Marie have two grown children and two grandchildren. He comes from a family of ten and he writes from his experiences in his stories for children.

His stories are written with a flow of rhyming sentences and are easy to read to children. His stories help to build children's confidence as they try to fit in with their peers in our society of today."

Joseph says, "Every child needs to discover his or her potential to their talents and uniqueness as well as adult encouragement and love."

MICHAEL AND ALICIA SMITH

Michael and Alicia Smith reside in Eastern Connecticut. Michael is an illustrator who works from home and cares for their son who was born with a disability. Alicia is an elementary level art teacher in Ledyard, Connecticut. They also have a daughter and they enjoy golf, gardening and working in the community during their leisure time.

How many bones can you find in this book?